This work is intended as purely fictitious in nature. It is a story told in a fantasy world. Any resemblance to people or situations is entirely coincidental.



Edited by: Abdelrahman A. E. Metwally

ISBN: 978-3-911111-15-7

First Paperback edition: March 2024

# Dedication

**For *Dr* Seif**

Through sheer perseverance, overcoming oneself, and force of will, you did it. I sit here in awe, knowing what you've had to endure to get to where you stand today, and I have only one thing left to say to a friend I miss dearly:

*Told you so.*

This one is for you.

There is much in this tale I think you might appreciate, but above all else, I'm certain you will foster a disdain for its main character that - if nothing else- we will both find genuinely amusing.

*"The most beautiful of ends are often paved in gruesome beginnings."*

To Nosfara
Bontara
The Ingvaki Desert
Desola
The Gaudy Coast
Celara
Contara
To Shorana
Map of
The Gaudy Coast

# I have no Respect

## 25th OF THIRD FALL 479 F.O.
## LORD FATHER & LADY MOTHER

I know what you did with **Nelyon**.

Was it because he was not of noble birth?

Was it because father did not like the breadth of his shoulders?

Or was it you, mother, who did not like the cut of his jib?

Or was it my dearest sister, who could not keep a secret?

He worked hard; he was honest and a fool. But he was my fool.

You have arranged suitors for me that treat me as a tool for progress; both of you have tirelessly scrounged the coast for any of noble birth that would fix your position in **Bontara**, I see that. You did not raise a dumb child, much to your own chagrin.

But to kill an honest, hardworking, well-meaning, loving fool?

Do not think for a moment that I believed your lies about scoundrels sinking his boat while he was at sea. In fact, I found his boat, and I will leave this place, never to return. Perhaps I will join the very scoundrels you claimed killed my love.

I have no respect for any of you. In fact, I have no respect for anything, not anymore, not after what you did. You've taught me time and time again that we were the best amongst our people. If that is true, then I would rather rot with those you think are our worst.

Farewell, though none of you deserve it.

***Paranessa**, no longer*

# For Royalty

## $10^{th}$ OF THIRD SUMMER 482 F.O.

"Lady **Liora**, is there nothing I can say to change your mind?"

Lady Liora sat on a round stool, quietly admiring the vast sea before her. A complete entourage of knights, lords, and ladies stood around her; their ship had long since departed, but none aboard could bring themselves to believe what they were doing.

High King **Alon**'s daughter, the fair Lady Liora, was departing **Migora** by the eastern city of **Nosfara**, in search of what she called, *'An adventure worthy of legend.'* And being the High King's daughter, she proved difficult to stop.

"I told you, Sir **Rork**." The proud princess addressed her knight protector, all the while neglecting to return his gaze. "If you do not wish to embark on this endeavour, then I will not begrudge you; and I will free you of my service should you desire."

Lady Liora would have been described as pleasant to behold, if only she could bear to smile. Her expression was ever haughty, her long straight hair dropped to her shoulders, tinting the golden weave of her gown with her dark brown hair. She was beautiful, of that no one had a doubt; but it would always be the way she looked at people that detracted from her beauty.

She was a princess; she knew it, and she would never hesitate to make people know it.

"My Lady, I am bound to your service as are we all," the knight attempted to reason with the unamused princess. "I do not fear for my life. I fear only what this adventure might bring."

He did not fear for his life. The knight did not lie; but he feared for his helplessness at sea.

Many of her entourage could not even find proper footing when a simple wave crashed against their ship. How was he to protect his princess when he could barely stand himself?

"Are you, or are you not, a capable protector?" She asked as a wave rocked the ship.

The skies remained clear, however unruly the sea might have been.

"The sea is treacherous, my lady," he continued, although he knew it was wasted effort to change the mind of a princess. "I fear that which I cannot protect you against."

"You fear too much," she decided. "Now go, all of you, leave me marvel at this sea that I have been deprived of in **Tunhil**."

"As you wish, my lady," Sir Rork bowed and abruptly left through the crowd of gathered lords and ladies. He muttered a few curses under his breath, but he would not stand idle. He walked across the deck of their modest ship and up towards the helm, where two peculiar men were. One stood over the wheel pensively, the other sat back in his chair, all too relaxed for the occasion.

"From your demeanour I gather the princess remains stuck in her ways?" The man at the helm asked.

Sir Rork could only nod in response.

"Spoiled brat," the other man said as he swung his chair back, crossed his arms behind his head, and rested his feet on the wooden rails around him. He seemed like a capable deckhand to Sir Rork, if lacking in all forms of mannerisms.

"I would beg that you refrain from using such language around her highness," Sir Rork uttered, "Or indeed in my presence."

The man laughed in response and looked up at the sky again.

"Tell me at least," Sir Rork was interrupted as he held onto the rails himself. Another wave rocked the ship, and the knight was completely shown to be out of place. "Tell me that no storms come, at least."

"None that we can predict," the deckhand replied, still calmly swinging in his chair.

"Good, that is at least good." Sir Rork calmed himself down, but the captain at the helm would have words.

"Good knight, forgive the question, but isn't there a war with Hydaria? How has the High King even allowed this?"

"A war our High Lord of War is handily winning."

"Are they fierce, these Hydarians?"

"Very, but fortune turns to favour us. I served for the first years of this war nearly six years ago, and it was far messier when it began."

"And now you guard a princess?"

"I do not care for your tone, captain. It is an honour to guard Lady Liora. In fact, the first Migoran Knights are royal protectors. Now perhaps you should focus on what was asked?"

"Forgive me, good knight," he started, "I believe your exact words were, *'Set off into sea, and remain as close to the coast without it being seen.'* Well, we've done that. Now how much longer are we to remain on this course? Or is there a course at all?"

"We shall remain on this course until the sea offers up an adventure to sate the princess' appetite." Sir Rork replied sternly, and immediately the captain shot him a questioning gaze. "Unless you know of a way we can make something exciting seem to happen."

"I could jump into the sea and pretend to be some legendary drowned prince she must have read about," the deckhand laughed.

"With your looks? You'd be whatever drowned the prince in the first place!" The captain yelled back, and both men laughed it off, much to Sir Rork's annoyance.

"We could pretend to shipwreck at a coast," the deckhand said, giving Sir Rork some glimmer of hope that these two men could be taken seriously. "A which point we seize the princess and show her a real adventure."

"Aye, with your ugly face to stare at, she won't be lacking for no adventures," the captain agreed and Sir Rork angrily smashed his fist into the rail to silence the laughter.

"I can see that neither of you gentlemen are particularly bright," he announced, his face fuming red. "Just keep us on course captain, the longer we remain out here, the better your reward shall be."

"We'll see to it, Sir Knight." The captain nodded and turned the wheel slightly as he noticed the paler colour of the coastal waters begin to show prominence. "We'll also be hoping not to run into any adventures, as disappointing for the princess as that might sound."

"For once we agree," Sir Rork said, but nothing that day would seem to go as the knight desired.

"Captain! Captain, a ship is approaching! And she's coming in fast." A man hastily made his way past Sir Rork, who shook his head and sighed.

"Surely it is not an uncommon occurrence for two ships to meet at sea, is it?" Sir Rork asked, but the ghastly face of the man told him this was no ordinary ship.

"Not when it's coming straight for us. She wants to ram us, captain!" The man cried. His voice was loud enough for most of the deck to hear and immediately chaos erupted. The Lords and Ladies that had come to accompany the princess out of duty were now completely out of place.

They panicked and rightly so.

"Full sail!" The captain roared as he turned the wheel to take evasive action, the man nodded and echoed the command as he ran back to the mast and immediately the modest crew of the ship got to work. However, behind the captain was laugher, Sir Rork could not understand why.

"You there! Why are you laughing?" He asked of the deckhand who remained in his seat, leaning back, "Is our peril so amusing to you?"

"Your peril is my peril, my lord." He laughed again, "Best ready that blade of yours. You'll have your hands full if it's her."

"Again? Do you actually believe she exists?" The captain said aloud as he tried to gauge the distance between the two ships and tried to measure the angle.

"Her? Who is she? What manner of myth has you sailors wetting your breeches? Tell me!" Sir Rork put a hand on his blade's hilt, which made the deckhand burst out laughing.

"Would you stop laughing and help?" The captain now cried. Even he seemed shaken by the speed of the ship he now saw clearly approaching. "Oh no, she isn't ramming. Clever, how very clever. All hands brace! Ready your blades, she means to board us!"

Another wave shook the ship, leaving Sir Rork grasping at the rails. The men all around were readying themselves for combat, the Migoran Lords and Ladies were all fighting for a place below deck, and then Sir

Rork saw her. Princess Liora was standing with both hands on the side rails, watching as the larger ship collided with their own.

"Brace!" The captain's voice rung, his own blade sung as he freed it from his scabbard; and the deckhand remained seated without a care.

Sir Rork could not find his feet.

The sea was not where he and his knights belonged. Here, his efforts were futile. He saw men and women jump from the other ship, brandishing their blades as carelessly as they did their unkempt faces. The knight finally managed to pull out his blade, and with the help of the rail, he made way towards the middle of the deck, where the princess would have been.

The fight that broke out made all the chaos of a battlefield seem orderly and tidy. Sir Rork could not tell friend from foe, nor could he see too far around him without a blade flashing in his face for him to parry; and as he postured to engage, his opponent would swivel away and find another target.

Sir Rork hated the sea, and all it had to bring. He could not even measure if a side was winning until he heard a distinct scream.

"Lady Liora!" He cried, and immediately the fighting died down. The Migoran princess was held by her hair, a blade at her neck, by a woman with the most curious violet hair.

"Unhand me!" The princess cried and the woman behind her smiled as she noticed the leverage now in her hands. A violent tug at the princess' hair was all it took to quiet her down for the time being.

"Well, well, it seems I've caught a quarry more valuable than gold or trinkets!" The woman behind the princess brought her head next to the princess'. "Smells nice too, well? Someone needs to start talking. Who do I have my blade round her neck? That is, if any of you value her life."

"No, please stop!" Sir Rork let out as he saw the blade sink against Liora's soft skin. "She is my daughter. Please unhand her!"

Rork lied, knowing he could not tell the wretched woman that she had caught a princess. His mind raced to make up the rest of his fable, but the treacherous woman moved first. She dragged the princess along with her as she walked over to the captain by the ship's wheel.

"Do keep your ship steady, captain," she teased and as she walked behind the captain, she bumped him into his own wheel. "Now, who are you? And more importantly what are you going to give me for this sweet lass?"

"I am Lord Rork," he let out hastily, trying to make anything up as he went, "I am a knight in High King Alon's service. He sent me south to send a message to **Contara**. And I beseech you, we have no valuables save for what vanities you see before you. Please, take it all, but leave my daughter alone."

"Oh, but if you are willing to part with this much, then there must be more!" The woman rejoiced and tugged harder on Liora's hair. She looked at the princess in agony and smiled lecherously. "We are going to be very good friends, aren't we, lass? What's your name?"

"Let me go!" The princess cried, scared and angry all at the same.

"What a horrible name," the woman mocked and kicked the nearby captain out of nothing but the fun of it. "You're the first person ever to make me feel good about my name! **Phatasma**, at your service, and if we're going to get you back to your frightened father over there, you are going to have to tell me more about this journey of yours."

"She is merely my daughter-" Sir Rork tried to take command of the conversation, but immediately he felt a heavy hand hit the back of his head. All around him, he realised his knights were being tied up, their weapons were being removed.

As Phatasma spoke, her men removed any threat they could pose.

"You have a tongue, do you not, let-me-go?" Phatasma mocked again, "How else would I have known your name, so please do talk?"

"My name is not let me go!" The princess cried, her teeth grit, she was infuriated. "And if you do not wish to die, you will unhand me and all these men, now!"

Sir Rork bit his tongue. He had always begged for the princess to behave better, but he could not believe it might cost her so dearly.

"This isn't a very good friendship is it?" Phatasma frowned and dug the blade harder on her neck, "I'm not letting you go, and you're not telling me anything. How about we try again? I've always been told to try to make things work, so here, I am Phatasma and I have this nice sword around your neck. Now who are you, and what valuables are you hiding?"

"You aren't a gracious person, are you?" Princess Liora replied, making Phatasma almost burst out laughing. "Stop it! I really mean it. If you don't unhand me now and leave us be, my father will be very cross with you. He'll order his men to find you, and he has no mercy for those who cross his children."

"Your father will find me?" Phatasma picked up her interesting word usage. She looked at Sir Rork and back at the princess. "As far as I'm concerned it's I who has found him. And as far as he's concerned, it's me who has any mercy to show, not him."

"Sir Rork isn't my father!" The princess let out, and her knight's heart sank. "I am Princess Liora, daughter of High King Alon, High King of Migora! Now, do you understand who you're dealing with? You ignorant, petty scoundrel!"

Just as she uttered her last words, Phatasma's blade slit her throat.

"Princess! No! Why?!" Sir Rork erupted and tried to break free to rush to his princess' side, but there was nothing he could do.

Phatasma let her body drop, blood gushing from the princess' throat. Her last expression would be that of utter disbelief, all semblance of power she once thought she had escaped her, along with her dear life.

"That's right, my dear princess," Phatasma said as she eyed the princess' lifeless body. Phatasma could not help but watch as blood trickled all over the steps to the helm, the gasps and shocked voices of all on board drowned out as Phantasma gazed at the thick blood puddling now at the foot of the steps.

"I am a petty scoundrel, aren't I?"

"That was High King Alon's daughter!" Sir Rork yelled again. He could not help the tears that escaped his eyes then, "He would have paid you! He would have given you more than you could have possibly asked for! *I* would have paid you! Why? Why did you kill her?!"

Phatasma leapt over the princess' corpse and held Sir Rork's chin as the surrounding men tightened their hold over him.

"Did I act too hastily? I'm sorry, I guess hostages aren't my forte." Phatasma mocked as she inspected Sir Rork oddly. "If it makes you, or your *High* King Alon, feel any better know that she was struck down by a queen."

"What manner of queen are you?!"

"The Queen of Scoundrels, of course," Phatasma flashed Sir Rork a smile before she brought her blade to his neck. His eyes flickered, his vision blurred as his teeth clenched. Yet he was not dead. He heard laughter and Phatasma pulled her blade away.

She was toying with them.

Lives were toys in her hands, and it repulsed him.

"Sir Rork, I have decided that you will live." Phatasma said.

She turned around and walked back up the few steps, beyond Liora's corpse. As wretched a woman as she was, her wanton allure was undeniable. She wore a merlot red velvet vest, unbuttoned brazenly save for a button near her waist; and her leggings were tight to complement her curvaceous look.

"I despise kings and queens, Sir Rork, which is why I claim to be one." She bent down and found an eye-catching feather in Liora's garments. "They think they own the world, and you who serve them all think the same. Give me more than I can ask for? Hah, I take what I want, Sir Rork. I will let you live to go tell your High King Alon how his daughter died. Maybe you will all think twice before venturing into the sea."

A deathly silence spread throughout the ship, as Sir Rork had nothing more to say. His eyes went blank, his lips twisted as he watched Phatasma pick up a feather and pluck it from Liora's garments and into her violet hair. Then she investigated the lifeless body and found a curio in the form of a parchment that she pilfered as well. The knight's stomach churned with disgust.

"How do I look?" Phatasma asked, but no one replied, and her expression soured. "What are you all waiting for? I said Sir Rork was to live, not the rest of them, send them to their princess. I have no use for nobles. And when I ask how I look; I expect compliments next time!"

The collective screams that echoed throughout the ship were spine shivering, but what was ghastlier was how quickly they were snuffed out. The entourage of nobles that had ventured out to sea at the behest of a princess' lust for adventure had all met their untimely ends.

"Do strip them of any valuables, of course. This is as fine a haul as we could have asked for," Phatasma announced and looked around the ship. "I've decided. We shall scuttle the ship and take her crew."

"Do you enjoy this?" Sir Rork spat. The scoundrels were content with his bindings and had left him to plunder from the dead bodies at their captain's command. "Do you think you control who gets to live and who gets to die? Just because we are out at sea?"

"I'd say I do yes," Phatasma looked back at Sir Rork. She pushed the body of the dead princess with her foot and then pointed at Sir Rork. "She dies and you live. Did I not say that would happen? And what does it matter if I enjoy this or not? I do only what I must."

"Must?! Must..." Sir Rork could not find the strength to argue. He did, however, find the courage to perform one last act of defiance. "Do as you see fit; however, you control nothing, even here at sea. I will not deliver my liege your message, nor will I live for your sake!"

Phatasma's eyes widened slightly as she watched Sir Rork push himself up, and in one last act the Knight flung himself from over the ship's rail. His armour weighing him down as he quickly sunk, drowning himself only to slight Phatasma. In his heart, he could not bear living with the shame of watching his princess die in front of him, and in his stubborn mind, he saw an opportunity to shame her murderer.

"What an insufferable man." Phatasma told herself as she heard laughter from behind her. She frowned and turned to face the deckhand, who had been sitting in his chair throughout all the events of that day. Leaning back, resting, as if he was detached from all that took place around him.

"Insufferable he might have been, but he did make a point," the deckhand said casually. "Looks like the Queen of Scoundrels cannot choose who lives and dies."

"Oh, can't I?" Phatasma plucked a dagger from her belt and threw it directly at the deckhand, who immediately reacted by letting his chair fall all the way back. And in a show of finesse, he found the dagger in the woodwork next to him, pulled it out, and turned to block Phatasma's second attempt. She had charged him herself in case he dodged her dagger throw, but she could not anticipate that he would be ready for her too.

"I couldn't help but overhear your conversation, Phatasma." The deckhand said as Phatasma let up; and the man immediately returned the dagger, hilt facing Phatasma. "Perhaps I can be a better friend than your last acquaintance?"

"You are an interesting man, go on, you already know my name," Phatasma inspected the unsightly dark-skinned man before her.

"**Desgar**, a pleasure to meet you, Captain."

## For Comrades

19th OF FIRST SUMMER 483 F.O.

Nights at sea were eerily quiet for Phatasma and her ship.

The star-studded sky above enveloped all as only the sound of waves crashing, ebbing and flowing around them echoed. Every night was as dark as the next. The pitch-black sea around them seemed ominous when calm, and murderous when aggravated. But such was the life they led, and times were pressing as always they were.

"Captain, we've been idle for too long," one rugged man said.

Phatasma had made it a habit to go below deck and see what her men were saying, if only to ensure their loyalty. She had no love for her crew.

To her, they were mere tools, as she might have been to them.

"And what'd you suggest, **Verto**?" Phatasma spat back. She was hunched forward on a barely held together wooden chair in front of the only table they had below decks. Food was laid out in scare quantities around the table. It was plain to any that they were struggling for supplies, and yet Phatasma sat in front of them all with an open vest and gold decorating her body. Circlets, bracelets, earrings, necklaces, anklets and even golden hair bands, even her eyes were changing colour, or so it seemed. She was every bit the decorated scoundrel everyone thought her to be.

"That we'd move back where the trade ships are, captain. Raid the next one we find!" Verto replied, who was barely clad at all. A belt, loose trousers and boots was all he could afford to throw over himself.

His suggestion, however, made the men around him nod, but Phatasma found herself stifling a laugh.

"Were you lot always this clueless? No, don't answer that. Or do, it might just amuse me." Phatasma toyed as she laid herself back in the creaking chair. She threw her arm over its back and reached for a half full flagon of ale. "Drink up. This is all the action we're getting for a while now."

"We didn't come out here to wait!" Verto yelled, challenging Phatasma's decisions openly. Hearing this made Phatasma glad she went below decks often. Having her men discuss things such as this among themselves without her would surely have led to a mutiny sooner or later. "This isn't what you promised us we'd be doing out at sea!"

"You didn't come out here at all, Verto," Phatasma yelled back, raising her voice louder than Verto. In a very primal way, she was stamping her authority on the ship. "I brought you all out here. In fact, I bought you all. Only thing I promised you lot was gold, and I see you have more of that than you know how to store it all."

"What use is gold if we can't dock?!" another man cried. Phatasma had indeed brought them riches they could not imagine ever attaining. But she also brought them infamy. Ever since they set out to sea, they were locked out to it. "You can't eat gold, captain, and you sure can't wear it either!"

"Excuse me?" Phatasma shook her earrings with her fingers, making them jingle annoyingly. She knew she was pushing her luck with their patience. Their sceptical eyes all fell on their captain as they contemplated her usefulness. Phatasma calmly sipped at the flagon and sighed as she set it down and stood up.

"Very well. I see I'm due to make you all another promise." She put one boot on the table and leaned forward, slowly eyeing everyone sat around her. From the corner of her eye she spotted Desgar, sitting far away, comfortably away from all the noise. He annoyed her with his attitude. He was the most capable man she had at her disposal, but she could not stand him since she picked him up.

"What promise would that be this time?" Verto demanded and looked back at Phatasma, "Are we finally getting back to raiding? Has the captain come to her senses?"

"I'll start by this promise," Phatasma locked eyes with Verto, "If you talk again without my permission, I'll have your tongue. There's my first promise."

There was some madness about Phatasma when she talked to her crew. A madness that dared them all to challenge her, a sort of subtle insanity that held them back, barely. But without promise of hope, even the maddest of insanities would not detain them much longer.

"And before you lot start chanting about it, you all want to get back to the trader's trail?" Phatasma spat to one side and looked at them again. "We never left the trader's trail, you bunch of clueless planks. It's they that have stopped coming. You all thought merchants would just keep coming at us like cattle? Do any of you understand what it means for us to keep attacking merchants the way we do? Of course not, let me spell it out, we are hurting Migora."

"Who cares about Migora?" A confused voice replied immediately, but Phatasma was quick to reply.

"You all should, because Migora is building ships." Phatasma announced with a stomp. She pushed both her hands on the table and eyed her crew menacingly. "Not lightweight flat bottom ships like this pile of heap, either. They're building proper warships. Three, to be precise, and the only goal of these ships is to catch us. Two of these ships will patrol the two major coastal cities, and the third, they call her *'Tulip's Tendrils'*. And her tendrils are out to get us. Whispers speak of a fourth as well, but ye didn't hear that from me. They want us all dead. But who cares about Migora? Any of you?"

The silence was just what Phatasma wanted to hear.

She grinned and tapped the wooden table.

"How do you know all this, captain?" Another man asked.

"It's my job to know all this because I'm your captain," Phatasma replied quickly. "I've made you all rich. I've fulfilled that promise already and you've all fulfilled your end of the bargain by letting me lead you. Now I'll give you all another promise, but I'll need something else from you in return."

They all looked up at Phatasma. She had somehow managed to wrap them around her fingers once more. Desgar watched from afar as Verto slowly capitulated to his charismatic captain, and Phatasma would not stop there.

"First the promise," Phatasma shook her hair freely for a moment. Her beauty captivated the hopeful crew for a moment; but Desgar saw through it, to Phatasma, her charms were but another weapon. Desgar silently began to wonder what manner of sea demon had he ended up serving. "All of you, bar none, shall be free of this ship and indeed the sea. You will remember then our old agreement issued a single box as big as you could carry to fill with treasure? Well, all of you have been generous with the size of these boxes, and I have been even more generous in filling them to the brim. You will all be allowed to keep these crates, you will all be allowed to keep your treasures, moreover I shall find a destination which will incriminate none of you."

"Too good," Verto snapped, "What'll you ask of us then? There's always something with you, captain, isn't there?"

Phatasma silently placed her flagon down and walked around the men until she was behind the seated Verto. All of her crew eyed her as she made her way to their vocal leader. She bent down behind him and threw her arms around him, pressing her chest seductively into his back.

"Verto, did you forget what I had told you?" Phatasma whispered into the man's flustered ears. The entire crew had known one thing about Phatasma, that she did not hesitate to act on her impulse or to prove a point.

Verto froze in fear at what Phatasma would do to him.

"I'll be taking this," she whispered again, and suddenly her hands darted to the man's trembling mouth. She yanked it open and with three fingers held Verto's tongue; the crew all turned away and began to feel their lips twist at what they knew Phatasma would do. But instead they heard laughter. Phatasma straightened her posture and wiped her hand on to Verto's bare shoulder.

"Captain?" His trembling voice asked.

"Your tongue is mine now, Verto. Do you understand?" She asked, and the man nodded despite of himself. Such was the power of hope. Phatasma had given them much to hope for and was now toying with them. However, she still wanted something from them, a show of loyalty. "Verto is right. I mentioned this would be a new accord. I shall ask something of you all, but this time I shall let you commit as much to it as you all want."

Phatasma let the men murmur amongst themselves for a few moments as she walked back slowly towards her chair. Her hand stretched out to glide all over the backs of the men she passed by. She would slip an inaudible whisper here, or an inappropriate giggle there, until she was back seated.

"What I want is simple," she started, but the men were still having conversations among themselves. "Your lives."

The words she uttered brought ghastly expressions to the faces of all who sat before her. Phatasma's demeanour and the way her eyes watched all of them back at the same time only amplified the terror of the moment. Until, however, Phatasma broke down into laughter.

"Forgive me, your captain is a petty woman," she admitted as she stopped herself from laughing. She did, however, manage to once again capture their undivided attention. "What I truly want might seem strange, but I shall ask it of you all the same. You are free to not partake at all, and I shall still deliver on my promise. Look at your treasure chests, men, and tell me, what is it that made us rich if not the sea? I might be mad to think of it this way, but I want to give back to the sea some of the treasure that it has shared with us. I ask of you to join me in this. Tonight I shall lift anchor and head out to the graveyard. Yes, to where we scuttle the ships we capture. And I shall give back to the sea some of my own gold, and I invite all of you to join me, with whatever gold you see fit to depart with. May the sea always bring us good favour!"

At that precise moment, the ship swayed and rocked by the sea; the wooden underbelly of the ship creaked and Phatasma started to move towards the ladder to return to deck.

She left them to ponder among themselves for a moment; Desgar watched and found himself amazed at how her rowdy crew eyed their gold with sorrow. Phatasma did not leave them for long however, her voice rung from above to remind them she would not go about the business of lifting anchor by herself.

Even the voyage to the graveyard of ships was quick and gave them no time to contemplate Phatasma's words. As quickly as they had raised the anchor, they found themselves dropping it again. Immediately Phatasma had the men bring out lit candles as she prepared her tribute to the sea.

"O bountiful sea that has given much to me, I praise thee and return my gold free!" Phatasma started, and stood dangerously on the side railing of the ship with a heavy chest full of jewellery she had handpicked. Phatasma closed the chest tight and let it drop, before she jumped back and turned to look towards her crew. Much to her pleasure, most of them had prepared offerings.

"O bountiful sea," the first of her crew came to the side of the ship as well, with two palms full of coins. "Take my gold and keep me safe."

Phatasma smiled at the attempt and nodded at the man as he passed by. The next few were silent and dropped wildly varying amounts of gold. Some were as miserly as to toss in a few coins, others full sacks worth.

But then, one man among her crew surprised her completely. He appeared from below deck with his entire chest in tow. He slowly made his way to the side of the ship and placed the chest on the side railing.

"O bountiful sea, much have you given to me," he said, trying to remember Phatasma's words, "For that and more I praise thee, and back to your clutches do I return your bounty."

With that, he pushed the entire chest off the side, filled to the brim with everything he had gained from this expedition. At the time Phatasma clapped to encourage him, but her eyes trailed off in thought as she saw the man's relieved face. This was a moment Phatasma would look back to, but she could not know it at the time.

No one clapped with Phatasma, no one wanted to follow his offering either, and so Phatasma thanked them and ended her sacrament.

"I promise you all that this has not gone to waste." Phatasma said, as the men pulled the anchor once again to return to the route they had been plundering. "Our course is set, and the winds are kind. This has been a taxing night on us all. Go rest, all of you. Your captain will stand watch this night, and I promise you that soon you shall all be free men!"

Her tired crew did not give a response. They had too much to think about as they turned in for the night. One that would prove fateful for Phatasma's crew of scoundrels. That night, the men were truly tired. Some thought they heard boots pounding along inside the deck, a telltale sign of someone stealing ale, but none of them could be bothered to check.

The night had been long and extremely eventful.

It was Verto that finally woke up hours later, only to cough as he inhaled a good portion of smoke. His eyes caught the blaze and quickly he jumped up to his feet and in disbelief watched as the lower decks flooded with fire and smoke.

"She lied to us!" He yelled, and slowly Phatasma's crew started to wake up. "She lied to us all!"

The crew awoke that day to realise what had become of their ship and their captain's promise. Her words echoed through their minds as the mixture of fear and rage filled their hearts.

*'All of you, bar none, shall be free of this ship.'*

And so the ship would burn around them.

*'You will be allowed to keep your treasures.'*

And they were, for all the good their gold did them then.

*'I shall make sure to find a destination which will not incriminate any of you.'*

And she did, for neither death nor the bottom of the sea would discriminate nor incriminate.

Of all the men present there, only Desgar had the courage to hide his face in his arms and run through the flames screaming.

"I should have kept one of them," Phatasma said to herself.

She lay on her back in a small boat she would use to travel from shore to her ship. Only now she had used the boat to escape the fire she started on her own ship. She had rowed herself all the way to the graveyard of ships where she was now diving to collect the treasure her crew had handily given the sea. "Maybe two, one to dive and another to row."

She sat up and looked at the oars wearily, and sighed. There was not even a hint of remorse in her voice for what she had done. Her crew were either being burned alive or drowning. The ship that had carried her would sink to the bottom of the sea by her own hand. Even the gold that her crew had given up to the sea as a tribute she had desecrated.

"Maybe three..." she let out as her eyes glazed over her almost bare, glistening, aching body. Phatasma barely clad herself in anything. Her clothes -which she refused to get wet- were neatly packed above her blade, next to the gold she had retrieved from the sea. The reason why she chose this place for a ship graveyard was because of how deceptively shallow it was, and so it was perfect to hide gold for easy retrieval as well.

Suddenly, a hand rose from the water and gripped at the side of the boat.

"What the?!" Phatasma kicked at the boat and pushed herself away from the hand. She looked around for her blade and quickly leapt for it, but as she pulled it from beneath her clothes and turned to face the intruder, she froze. "Impossible... Desgar?"

"Yes..." The dark-skinned man threw himself on his back in her boat. His body was giving up on him. "Captain... at your service."

Phatasma kept looking at Desgar in shock. She set down her blade and crawled up towards him. Her eyes did not stop widening as she inspected the man she had left to die, along with so many others.

"Are you... alone?"

"Yes, captain," he said, out of breath. "Your promise... was fulfilled."

"Not quite," Phatasma said as she eyed Desgar. "Tell me, why did you come here? Did you know I would be here?"

"I had a hunch." He closed his eyes, barely able to catch his breath or let his muscles rest.

"Then... why did you return to me?"

Desgar's ugly face twisted as he laughed and coughed up sea water.

"You aren't good at making friends, captain. I didn't want you to lose the only one you might have made."

Phatasma did not understand what Desgar saw in her in all this, but she had nothing but respect for the man then. She was far from being a good enough person to let this change her in the slightest, but she found appreciation for men driven by that she did not understand.

"Well, are you going to slack off now? Row with me. We need to get to shore! I haven't been back in years now!"

Desgar shook his head and could only laugh.

# For Kin

## 25th OF FIRST SUMMER 483 F.O.

The sun peeked its rays through cracks in the roof of the hovel she had commandeered, which made her cover her face with one arm as she slept.

"How could one so vile sleep so soundly?"

"Quiet. If she hears you, we're all dead."

It was there in a hovel off the coast of **Desola** that she had spent the last few days with Desgar. The hovel belonged to two brothers, orphans by the looks of them, and so Phatasma spared them. She did, however, tie them up and claim she would borrow their home for a while.

"Captain, I bring news."

Desgar barged in and Phatasma could only toss in her sleep.

"Taverns, inns, storehouses, the entire town, and coast. All of it's the same captain. No one's left that's interested in seafaring."

"Impossible." Phatasma muttered as she stretched, then pushed herself up and looked at the two tied up brothers. "Remind me to bring you two a real bed. This is crude, even for me."

Both of them had learned to remain silent, at the cost of a few scars they did not think would come their way.

"It's as I say, captain. Even offering double what you told me, all the good men are taken."

"You want your captain to repeat herself, Desgar? Impossible. Even if it's that **Fennyor** I keep hearing about, he couldn't have recruited *everyone.*"

"You be right, captain. He may be responsible for half the men we thought should be there."

"Half? What, is he manning a fleet?"

"Never was good at counting, captain."

"Remind me again why I kept you?"

"Me charm, captain."

Phatasma was too groggy to make any witty response, no matter how fertile Desgar's response was to snarky replies. She moaned and found her feet still unimpressed with her surroundings and more so with these tidings.

"Next time I tell you to go find me recruits, do so..."

"Of course, captain." Desgar laughed, and again she frowned. He was the one man she could not fully figure out, not yet. Perhaps that was why she had kept him after all, perhaps that was his charm.

Phatasma shuddered at that thought and extended a hand towards Desgar expectantly, and he understood. Desgar took out a small hexagonal black box and placed it into Phatasma's outstretched hand.

"At least you found my ointment."

"Say, captain, been meaning to ask," Desgar started as Phatasma opened the box and dipped her index into it. Only to scurry around the hovel in search of a mirror amongst her hoard, and when she found one, she applied to ointment. To her open eyes. "This be the recipe you found off the princess?"

Phatasma stopped and narrowed her eyes at Desgar.

"I liked it more when you were dumber."

Desgar laughed and brought the two tied brothers a drink as Phatasma finished treating her eyes.

"How do I look?" She asked.

"As treacherous as the sea, captain."

Phatasma rolled her eyes and blinked a few times. Clearly, the ointment stung, but she was committed to it. The Queen of Scoundrels sighed and stood in front of her makeshift mirror again and loosened her top. Phatasma was very deliberate with which buttons she opened and how she shaped her vest. She plucked a few different necklaces, bracelets, rings and earrings from her hoard, which she decorated herself with, then turned to exit the hovel.

"Stay guard, you two. We won't be long."

She mocked them as she dragged Desgar out of the hovel and marched towards the town.

"So? You said half were taken. What about the rest?"

"Seems they found honest work."

"Doing *what*? These coastal cities are barren of well-paying honest work. Good pay has ever been at sea, so what changed?"

"Aye, it's at sea still, captain. Someone's been investing into fisheries, fishing ships, charting expeditions. Didn't gather much of details, captain. All I know is they didn't want me gold."

"There's one tavern I know that's never let me down."

"Which would that be, captain?"

*'The Glittering Star'* was indeed not a tavern one could hope to find easily. And yet it was incredibly busy. The coast around Desola was not a simple beach. That was for the town itself. Surrounding it were many cliffs and headlands. And it was in a nook between such headlands and in a cave that overlooked an islet, that they found Phatasma's favoured tavern.

"How did you find this place, captain?"

"A woman needs her secrets, doesn't she, Desgar?"

"Not you, captain, at least not by the looks of you." He laughed, and she shook her head as she led them both towards the entrance with brazen confidence.

A burly man stood by the cave entrance, and there seemed to be two pathways behind him. Both were well lit by torches and spiralled inwards out of sight.

"Sun's too bright for any stars, don't you think so, starfish?" The burly man said, and Desgar turned to Phatasma immediately.

"Never too bright for a star that glimmers," Phatasma replied.

To which the man nodded over his right shoulder, where Phatasma led Desgar into the pathways beyond.

"Starfish? Captain?" Desgar laughed.

"Not fond of your tongue, are you, Desgar?"

The man continued to laugh, but Phatasma did not reach for any of her many hidden daggers. She did not brandish her sword or lay a finger on Desgar. She simply found him amusing, and perhaps she wished to understand his loyalty still.

Phatasma knew her way around the winding passageways of this cave system. They branched in many places, but she knew which turn to take each time. Eventually, the sound of laughter and singing could be heard, and then they both knew their way. The path to the Glittering Star was clear, from narrow corridors to wider chambers they emerged, and before them an establishment was built into one side of the cave.

"How do you know to get here, captain?"

"I followed a starfish, of course."

The door was open, not that anyone inside would have heard had they broken it down. The interior of the makeshift tavern was massive, more so than Desgar could have expected, and more than Phatasma could have recalled.

On one side, into a carved-out section of the cave, a bar was built. And it was stocked to the brim with kegs, barrels, and bottles of all shapes. It covered one edge of the inside, and before it was a great hall of many floors. A single central gap remained open on all floors, providing a precious view port to a platform at the ground level where all forms of entertainment took place. Four sets of spiralling staircases connected the floors of this tavern at their corners. Stairs which made it all the way to the very top of the tavern, and there hung a chandelier of many candelabras. On each floor, there was a litter of tables and chairs. No apparent attempt at organisation had been made at all, it would seem.

The most striking thing about this establishment, however, was the blatant spread of weapons along the inner walls in the form of open crates. Scimitars, longswords, bows and arrows, polearms, maces, morning stars, and cudgels. All in various states of disrepair. And the people inside mirrored the state of their establishment. They were rough and coarse for the most part. Most of them were dark-skinned and most of them looked mighty. But between the sea of grime danced a few soft faces. Fair-skinned women clad in mock gold dresses, clearly an imitation of Migora's golden weave. They pranced from table to table and collected Lots just for spending a moment or two with their patrons.

Desgar's eyes lit up.

"Captain, why? Why haven't you told me about this place?"

"Why? You'd never leave, Desgar."

Phatasma dragged Desgar towards a table that clearly had a few drunkards sitting around it. Three men they were, and they looked up at Phatasma and were ready to either shoo her away, or whistle her onto the table. But as soon as they realised who she was, two of them fell off their chairs and the other scampered away.

"Sit and watch, Desgar."

Desgar did as he was bid, but he couldn't help steal a glance at how Phatasma's visage alone steered away men he thought he'd need to scuffle with.

"Scoundrels of the star!" Phatasma yelled as she made her way to the central platform. One foot in front of the other as she walked, one hand on her hip, and the other brandishing a sword about.

Her voice echoed as she repeated her call once on the platform, and the band that had been singing immediately scurried away at the sight of her. The tavern fell silent, and all eyes were upon her.

"You lot are sat here wasting while the sea calls," she called out to them. "I've answered its call, and look what it has blessed me with!"

Phatasma stuck her sword into the floor of the platform beneath her and took off her rings and bracelets, only to toss them out and around various tables.

"Crates upon crates of treasure, riches beyond my wildest dreams, a hoard that rivals that of Migora, and why should it not, when I am a queen?"

"Sea bless ye with that body too?" A coarse man jeered from a nearby table as he greedily scooped up some of what she had tossed about, until he felt a dagger pierce the side of his mouth at a cruel angle. The man fell and made excruciating sounds as he clawed at his face, the blow as not immediately lethal, but soon would be.

"Why've ye come, Phatasma? Lost yer last crew?" Another asked from a few floors above.

"Dear me, no. They're right where I left them. All of them are richer than they dared imagine, all of them are with their own hoards. Just as I had promised them. Ask any of them, and they won't say any different."

A troubled silence took over the establishment, interrupted by the stabbed man's constant gruesome pleas for aid.

"A queen I may be, but I serve as do we all. I serve the sea, that much you all know as I've claimed to ye before. And it speaks to me in return. It tells me to venture deeper, to grow more ambitious, to carve an empire on the waves! And for that, I need more than the crew I possess. The sea calls to me as it does to all of ye. Who here would dare heed its call? Who here would follow me to crest the waves in search of more riches? I've come only to share my hoard, but only for those brave enough to follow."

A small cheer echoed from some of the higher layers, but far fewer than Phatasma had hoped for. Louder still was the moaning man, begging, clawing, searching for aid.

Phatasma grimaced and leapt off the platform to run her sword through his neck, if only to silence the inconvenience she had created. And no one dared or cared to interrupt her.

"Times have changed, Phatasma." One said from a floor above.

"If the sea speaks, you're not its only voice." Another said.

Phatasma pounced back onto the platform and looked upwards at the open section of the floors above.

"Explain yourselves! Have I not been the sea's loudest voice?"

"All who follow you seem to never return. You say they be stuck out at sea, but what good would that do us? We've found *honest* work, a fool like you that speaks for the sea, but lets us live on land."

"Honest?! Hah!" Phatasma made no effort to hide her scorn. "You are all nothing but rats, hiding in caves, stealing, thieving, scheming. What manner of *honest* work could any of ye possibly do? And who is the utter fool that promised it? Fools that you are for believing them."

"**Harvggad**'s own woman!" One man said, and the words echoed into Phatasma's head.

***'Marinarma.'***

"She set us to work on a ship far greater than any ye claim."

"Put us up to explore the sea, more than ye ever did."

"Sure, some of us fish and haul things around, but others find pearls and treasures at the bottom of the sea that don't need stealing."

"And she lets us live as we please!"

"Yer all still here in caves, damn it." Phatasma challenged.

"Times have changed, *Queen*. We may be unruly still, but Harvggad has turned a new leaf. This be a recognised establishment. Yer a season late, and crates of Lots short, Phatasma."

Phatasma shot a look to Desgar, who immediately knew to get up and make for the door, then Phatasma slowly leapt off the platform again and made for the stairs. The tavern watched, bemused with what she would do next, as she just kept climbing floor after floor.

"It be recognised alright, captain, they're here!" Desgar yelled as he, too, ran for the stairs.

*'Maybe this is why I keep him, he understands how I think. Either way, Migoran soldiers in pursuit is the last thing I needed, but perhaps I can turn it to my tide.'*

"You know what to do! And the lot of ye, don't be fooled by *honest* work. Honest folk are more crooked than any of ye! You'll see!"

With that last proclamation, she tossed another dagger at one door on the third floor where she had been, before climbing further still. Desgar noticed and went through that door, taking Phatasma's cue well. Leaving his captain to work her magic.

She reached the top most floor and that was when Migoran soldiers barged into the tavern, yelling for people to remain still. She was too far out of sight for them to notice.

"If it's me yer looking for, I be right here, ye dogs of land!"

She drew as much attention to herself as she grabbed onto the rails that guarded the open section in the middle of the top floor where she had been. Then she flung a few trinkets she had carried with her onto the soldiers below, and the greedy men of the tavern immediately jumped for them.

The soldiers were on the platform fending off greedy men from all around them.

*'Right, enough time for what needs doing, and they know where I be heading. Time to pay you a long overdue visit, Mari.'*

It took Phatasma a moment to find a rope she had been searching for. Gladly, she cut it and clasped onto it with both hands and it sent her flying high into the ceiling. There, she clutched onto an open hatch as the chandelier fell upon the soldiers and men below.

The hatch was located directly above the chandelier, and it led up into the front facing section of the tavern, part of the town proper. She knew where it would lead, but she had never needed to make the journey up in such a manner.

It was a storage room that she emerged into, or rather a crate that was placed atop the connecting hatch to hide it. From which she emerged and closed it again.

*'I knew this would come in handy. Now to get to Mari. Three daggers left. Should be plenty.'*

She remained completely silent in her movements, stifling any jewels that tried to chime. She moved from the storeroom into hallways that connected kitchens with stairs, but then she paused.

*'They'll never find me... ugh, this is such a flawed plan. But perhaps I can improvise.'*

Phatasma sat on the bottom steps of the staircase. She took out her sword and looked at her palm and sighed. With a wince, she cut through her own palm, only wanting a flow of blood. Then she put her palm over her vest near her waist and made it seem as though she had been stabbed. Then she waited for a few moments until finally she found what she was looking for.

"Excuse me, you shouldn't be here,"

It was a young girl that found her, a helper at the tavern.

"H-help..." she muttered and took her hand off her waist.

"What happened?! Stay there! I'll get help!"

The girl vanished, and so too did Phatasma. She tied her hand up firmly with a piece of cloth ripped from her vest, then marched upstairs with one goal in mind.

Marinarma's room was simple enough to find, and easier still to slip into, and of course the woman was there. Resting in her bed with one lit candle in an otherwise dark room, and a tome in her hands that she had been reading through.

*'You were always the better of us... so why is it that you now get in my way? I left you everything there was to leave.'*

"Just what is it you think you're doing, sister?" Phatasma demanded and stood there in the dim candlelight, startling her sister.

"Para? Oh my goodness, are you alright?!"

"Shut it, tell me. Tell me now, Mari. What do you think you're doing?"

"Para, calm down. Are you hurt?"

"Ask one more time and it'll be *you* who's hurting. Yes, Mari, I'm hurt. I'm hurt that my sister would follow in my footsteps for no reason other than to get in my way!"

"But... but sister, I only did what I thought was right. The way you spoke, the way you talked to me. Did you not think I was listening? Or did you think I was too dumb to understand? I felt it too, that call of the sea... but you know how I am. I can't go out there the way you do."

*'Oh I know, your porcelain white skin, your condition that has you pampered wherever you go. Why couldn't you have just stayed at home? You'd have made a fine present for some petty lord.'*

"Paranessa, I did not mean to hurt you." Marinarma said, then put away her tome and pushed herself to her feet slowly.

*'You've even coloured your hair like I did...'*

She was indeed extremely similar to Phatasma, only far more thinly and pale of skin. They both owned beautiful faces and were alluring for different reasons.

"Then why is it that I can't find people to recruit? Hm?"

"Sister, we've talked about this! I told you that you'd be safe here for a time, and you knew I was working to your same goals, but in a way that doesn't result in infamy for all those involved."

"I did not think you would actually deprive me of my one resource! You are doing this to spite me, aren't you? Your goals are so lofty, so noble, as to cure the deluded Paranessa, are they not? You're worse than *them*!"

"They cared for you!"

"They killed him!"

"That's not true, and you know it!"

A faint knocking came on the door, and Mari's normally white face grew paler still. Phatasma caught a glimpse of this, but snuck back into a corner of the room behind the door and next to a wardrobe.

"Mother, I heard screaming." A young boy walked into the room, no older than six years of age. And as he did Phatasma unwrapped her bandage.

*'Mother?! She's even adopting now?'*

"I-it's alright, nothing's wrong-"

She couldn't finish the sentence before Phatasma had lunged, closing the door and tackling the boy hard to the ground. Her dagger in her right hand and her left on his back.

Blood stained the back of the boy's shirt.

And he did not make a single motion.

Marinarma shrieked.

"Why?! Para! You monster!"

"I told you, sister. I told you I would hurt you."

Phatasma stood up, and walked slowly towards her sister, dagger in hand still.

"You are no sister of mine! You are a cruel woman! Do you wish so badly to be called a scoundrel?! Have you taken all leave of your senses?! Curse you, Phatasma, curse you! You are a poisonous seed in this world, Phatasma, and naught but poison will ever come of you! No man would ever have you, and should you bear child then know that they will never be yours, never will you be called a wife, and never will you be called a mother. Rot at sea Phatasma, rot there where fish slumber, for even they would fly away in disgust at your sight-"

With one hand, Phatasma embraced her sister, and with the other, she dug a dagger deep into her heart, and she brought her lips to her dying sister's ears.

"I'll take care of the boy. Sleep, sister. You won't be forgotten."

Marinarma fell to her knees, but her eyes widened at Phatasma's words. She fixated her gaze on the boy, which Phatasma flipped on his back, to see that he was still breathing. She had not stabbed the boy, she only made it seem as though she had. Her wounded hand placed on his back left a deceitful mark of blood upon his shirt, but Phatasma had merely stained it.

A wounded expression remained on Marinarma's face. She extended a hand weakly to the unconscious child, then fell, face first, into the ground.

*'Today, goodness died. No. It died four years ago.'*

But Phatasma's task was not yet done. She heard boots climb the stairs hastily, so she quickly locked the door, opened a window, then picked up the child and placed him on the bed before she hid once more.

She waited with bated breath, as Migoran soldiers broke through the door. Four of them there were, and as soon as they invaded the room they stopped.

"You two, search the room! You, with me."

Two of them went to examine the body, and the other two naturally went for the open window. Then Phatasma struck, one dagger after the other, keeping only the dagger with which she had stabbed her sister to herself.

Her daggers struck their marks, and two more men were added to the tally, but she had to take out her sword for the last two.

"There!"

Phatasma did not wait. She darted out of the room, but as soon as she did, she stopped and turned and remained close to the wall. The two men inside gave chase. They emerged from the room with significant momentum, only for the first one to find a sword thrust through his chest as Phatasma took him down to the floor. Fortunate as she was that town guardsmen were not as well armoured as Migorans out at war.

However, that was where her plan ended. She scampered to her feet, but the other guard was upon her. A hasty block left her on her back, knocked into a wall. The man was determined, and he continued his assault by kicking her into the wall. Phatasma dropped her sword and clasped onto the boot with wide eyes, in pain at the bone crushing shunt she'd received.

But as soft on the eyes as she'd appeared, her life at sea had taught her to be ruthless, even on her own body. She clasped his foot with both hands and kicked with both feet on his other leg, sending the man to the ground. Phatasma pranced up and ran back into the room as soon as she did. Inside she had two objectives, first she plucked the daggers out of the soldiers she had killed and placed them in their hands, then she turned to the child. The soldier, meanwhile, gathered his wits and approached the room slowly.

"Stay back!" She screamed as the man saw her clutch onto the boy with her lone remaining dagger around his neck.

"Filthy scoundrel, don't you dare!"

The man backed away, measuring for an opening, but Phatasma did not give him a chance. She tossed the boy's body at the panicked guard, who dropped his sword to catch the boy, only for Phatasma to pick it up and slice his throat.

The boy was safe still, so she plucked him out of the dead guard's hands and rushed downstairs, her mind racing now.

"Paranessa?" A familiar voice stopped her as she reached the bottom of the stairs.

*'Oh no... not him... wait, unless...'*

"Harvggad! These soldiers! They're brutes!"

"Calm down. What happened?"

There before her stood a beast of a man. His skin was well tanned, his magnificent beard was wide and his well-built body was more suited to wrestling wild boards than managing a tavern. There was a man that was well respected by scoundrels and lawmen alike.

"They killed her! It's all my fault... In the dark, they couldn't tell us apart... Mari is dead!"

"They did *what*?" Harvggad's eyes darkened, and he took ominously heavy steps towards the stairs.

"Wake up Harvggad! These are the savages you serve. They cannot tell friend from foe! They already took my sister, don't let them take me as well. I beg you."

"Get out of my way, woman."

Phatasma lifted the boy to his face and stood firm. As the sound of more boots came from the other rooms, more soldiers were on the way.

"I saved your son. Does that mean nothing to you?"

"Damn it, woman, I'm trying to help you! Get out of my way and follow me, and say not a damn word. Curse the day you returned, Paranessa."

Phatasma blinked, then clutched onto the child as she followed Harvggad upstairs. Betting on her lie, and on the honest simplicity of her sister's husband.

The massive man did not slow down until he reached Marinarma's room, then he fell to his knees next to her and he froze entirely.

*'Careful Harvggad, or it's you next.'*

"They're coming..." she whispered to the sound of more boots.

Harvggad put his wife's body in bed, and wrapped her up gently. Then he turned to face Phatasma with fire in his eyes. The next wave of soldiers was almost upon them, and Phatasma began to truly feel cornered.

Then Harvggad embraced her along with his child, and he turned in such a way that only her hair would be seen for anyone entering the room.

"Two dead!" a soldier yelled from outside. "That broken door, through there!"

Then they barged in, and Harvggad turned his head to face them and immediately he barked.

"What are you waiting for?! She escaped through the window, after her!"

"You heard him, lads, search the town! She won't escape us this time!"

Mercifully, they streamed out of the room, and as soon as they did, Harvggad took his son from Phatasma's clutches and pushed her into the wall.

"This is the gratitude I get for saving your child?"

"Do not dare test my patience. I've already repaid you."

"Then how about I repay you for a change, hm?"

Harvggad went to sit on the bed next to Marinarma's body, cradling his son, and lending Phatasma an ear.

"Mari and I both shared dreams," she started. "I know she would have been out at sea if her body allowed, and now they've taken even her ability to dream. I aim to do two things from here on out, two promises to myself and her. To live out the dream we shared to completion, for I already know how I can get to it. And to avenge her death, she was an innocent, loving woman. She cared for everything, even me, who so many have cast off as incorrigible."

"I fail to see how this repays me, Paranessa."

"Paranessa died a long time ago, the last traces of her died today."

"Then what is it you want of me, *Queen of Scoundrels*?"

"Your service, your men, and your wife's ship."

"You are a fool."

*'And yet, you have the eyes of a man with nothing to lose.'*

"I'll wait for you at *Marinarma's Ambition*."
"What?"
"My new ship. You know where it is."
*'I told you, Mari. You won't ever be forgotten.'*

# For Accords

## ~3rd OF FIRST SPRING 483 F.O.

Seasons had passed since Marinarma's death, and ever since then Phatasma had once again found her way out to sea. On the ship her sister had built, and with her sister's husband as a quartermaster, and with men that were once promised honest work to man her ship.

In fact, she had gained notoriety and infamy over the past few seasons, and this time, Desgar talked her into keeping the men she had at her disposal. Opting to grow her fleet instead of more sea tributes. Of course, she claimed that this was always her plan, but Desgar knew better than to believe that, and even better than to object.

Alongside *Marinarma's Ambition*, she had three more ships; the rest being much smaller in make. All under her command, but for the time being, she let the captains of these ships operate mostly autonomously. Leaving them each to pillage different regions of **The Gaudy Coast**, but they coordinated with each other to allow sea trade to grow. Some of them even began acting as enforcers to protect traders from the rest of Phatasma's fleet.

The Queen of Scoundrels finally had a realm of her own. She learned of more coves along the shore, and of more refuges further south. But she also gained a growing rival in Captain Fennyor.

Things came to a point that Phatasma herself rarely needed to intervene with raiding merchant ships. She kept herself for potential clashes with Fennyor, or the many smaller names that began cropping up, and with Migoran naval vessels.

It was on an idyllic early spring day that news of just such a vessel reached her, and quickly she took to plotting.

"This does not sit well with me, captain." Harvggad said.

Her quartermaster was the single most respected man across her entire small fleet. Thus, she gave him special allowances when disagreeing with her, but now she could not tolerate it. Not when her three other captains were gathered with her.

"Is that worry I hear? Value your life over her memory?"

Harvggad gave her a cruel look, but Phatasma continued.

"The ship carries five crates of fine Migoran Gold Weave, perhaps two or three villages' worth of produce. Credit to Captain **Norlac** for this vital information." Phatasma threw her arm around the man in an unsettling manner as she spoke, and Desgar whistled from afar, further adding to the awkwardness.

Captain Norlac was not as most scoundrels. He was far more refined and reserved a man than their likes. That, and he owned a proud golden Hydarian mane of hair. He claimed to have been a Quartermaster in Ragos' army that deserted following a certain defeat at the hands of Mithra. His only refuge as a Hydarian in Migora, he found, was among scoundrels, but his organisational skills gave him a lofty place among them.

"And thanks to Captain **Myures**, they think their newfound route will avail them." Phatasma left Norlac and continued to walk behind the gathered men, this time leaning herself into Myures, who welcomed the company. There was a man whose skin was darker than any, and whose physical hardiness surpassed most. His claim was that he came from a clan living in the desert, and he had been one of the oldest well-known scoundrels in the Gaudy Coast. Having him pledge allegiance to Phatasma was a massive boon to her recruiting capabilities. The man's reputation served her well, and his experience even more so.

"Thanks to him, their newly minted route appears to have gone unnoticed by us. He has even guarded it himself with his own ship from errant scoundrels. Which leaves us with you, Captain **Dengal**."

Phatasma moved over to him now, and jumped to sit on the table, leaning to one side to face him ominously. They were all unhinged in their own ways, but Phatasma excelled at unsettling even the most notoriously deranged of them.

"Aye, captain." Dengal's coarse voice scraped at her ears as he spoke. "The accord with Fennyor remains. The *King's Route* is to be cultivated for later plundering."

Dengal had once served Fennyor, but Phatasma's more recent string of successes helped sway him over to the Queen of Scoundrels. His notoriety came from operating further south. Where trade was more sparse, but so too was the competition.

"Yes, you've done brilliantly with your former captain." She said, then picked up a parchment from next to her. The contents of which did not matter in the slightest to her. "The thing with accords at sea... you're best breaking them before they break you."

She ripped the paper, and Harvggad rolled his eyes.

"Captain Fennyor will be furious if we do," Dengal said.

"Exactly!" Phatasma clapped him on the shoulders and leapt off the table to find her position at its head. "That ship's bounty is worth seeing his irate face, and the pain to Migora will ease the loss of Mari."

"Nothing we say will change your mind, captain, that much we know. So what may your plan be? Surround the ship and demand they give up their wares? Board it? Ram it?" Harvggad suggested.

"Should just sink it and fish the crates." Myures said.

"And ruin the weave?" Dengal snorted.

"Captain, I assume we were not brought out for consultation." Norlac said, in his usual calm demeanour that so wildly contrasted his peers.

"You were not, but it is amusing to listen to simpletons."

"Amusing, are we?" Dengal fumed, and just as he turned to face Phatasma, he felt a dagger pressed to his neck, to which he raised his hands.

"Growing more amusing by the second." Phatasma shot him a venomous glance, then pulled the dagger back and swapped it for an arm over the confused man's shoulder. "Relax, captain. I'm well on my way to granting you riches beyond your wildest dreams."

"Then why've you gathered us, captain?" Myures asked.

"To listen, and to obey. Eyes with me, this is what we'll do."

It took an entire regiment of men working in synchrony just to navigate the sea, and Phatasma's newly acquired crew were only just gathering their bearings as they voyaged along. Phatasma found her crew would conjure up tunes to synchronise their work. Sometimes they even made sense.

*Oh, with gold I sailed and docked at port*
*And there they asked what I missed most*
*To sea I turned and pointed toward...*
*The feistiest crew on the gaudy coast!*

*Cause we're the feistiest crew on the gaudy coast!*
*In dance or song, no right, no wrong*
*The feistiest crew on the gaudy coast!*

*Oh, to tavern I went, no food there short*
*And there they asked what I ate most*
*Looked at me bowl and said from heart...*
*The liveliest stew on the gaudy coast!*

*Cause it's the liveliest stew on the gaudy coast!*
*It moves it wiggles, I've seen it jiggle*
*The liveliest stew on the gaudy coast!*

*Oh, got caught one night in nobleman's court*
*And there they asked if I were lost*
*Of course I was, I missed me cart...*
*The flightiest scow on the gaudy coast!*

*Cause it's the flightiest scow on the gaudy coast!*
*Through wave and storm, she kept us warm*
*The flightiest scow on the gaudy coast!*

*Oh, I found meself at gallows fort*
*And there they asked what I'd dared boast*
*To sky I looked and could see in part...*

*The sightliest view on the gaudy coast!*

*Cause she's the sightliest view on the gaudy coast!*
*Her violet hair, her air, her flair*
*The sightliest view on the gaudy coast!*

*Oh, I opened me eyes and there I was...*
*With feistiest crew*
*And liveliest stew*
*On flightiest scow*
*All for the sightliest view on the gaudy coast!*
*The sightliest view on the gaudy coast!*

She let them have their fun, and was doubly pleased when they sung her praises as well. But for now, as she stood at the helm of the ship, she remained focused.

There was a predatorial gaze in her eyes that were slowly turning more violet by the day. Of her many mood swings, the hysterical glare she wore before raids was a clear sign as any for all to steer clear of her. She had one hand on her hilt, her fingers tapping methodically upon it, one after the other. The other hand she left to rest upon her wheel, then she shot a gaze to one side of her, then the other.

Starboard of her ship was *'Hida's Revenge'*, Captain Norlac's ship, with its telltale flag of a woman with blood for hair. Portside, she spied *'The Golden Heron'*, Captain Dengal's vessel. Flying a fake Gold Weave crane upon black sails.

Both paled compared to her Marinarma's Ambition.

In terms of armaments, there was also little room for comparison, where Phatasma had altered their ships to suit her needs. She had them build a tower around their ships' masts for archers to use as they approached. Around the base of these towers, she also had them build a wider compartment, which she would use to hide melee combatants before they were to board.

And while these additions had improved their fighting capacity, it had a negative impact on their manoeuvrability in deeper waters. Not that she had any need for her subordinates to tread deeper waters, not yet.

On her own ship, she had fitted two siege engines, mangonels capable of flinging rocks a fair distance away. They had been made lighter for use at sea, and she had cruelly allotted her two companion ships the task of carrying spare munitions for them.

Missing from their entourage was *'The Sea of Dunes'*, Captain Myures' ship, and the only one on a similar level with her own. And this absence was by design. Phatasma had identified a narrow route between a rock formation and coastal cliffs that traders had taken to using to avoid her scoundrels.

She had it on good authority that her quarry would pass through just this passageway. So she had stationed her ship along with the two by her sides to greet them when they made it through, and Myures to intercept them if they aimed to flee.

"Ready to fire, captain!"

Phatasma did not stir, her eyes fixated on the narrow gap from which she expected a vessel to appear. Her eyes had an uncanny quality about them, as though wherever she focused she could see with no need for a looking glass. Many wrote it off to luck, few ever linked Phatasma's forced colouration of her eyes to any real uncanniness, save for in pleasant superstition.

"Hold men!" she growled, and the wind was taken out of their sails. Hers as well, as she visibly grit her teeth at the sight that now emerged from between the narrow gap.

"What do you see, captain?" Harvggad asked, standing near.

"Full sail! Looks like Captain Myures cares not for my plans."

Only when they approached did they understand what she meant, as they saw two ships approaching, not just one.

The Migoran vessel had surrendered.

"What is the meaning of this?" Phatasma demanded, and heedlessly leapt onto the Migoran vessel when her ship was vaguely close enough.

Immediately, all Migorans aboard lifted their weapons, and Phatasma obliged. She aimed a sword at one man's neck to her right, and brandished a dagger, ready to be thrown at a man to her left.

Everyone froze stiffly at the sight of this mad woman's approach.

"No need for hostilities!" a man's voice came. "Allow me to make introductions. I am Lord **Lennaz Mer'Ginliya Ral'Throia**, a Migoran Baron, if you will, your highness."

The man had a refined look about him, but he was too fit to be a noble in Phatasma's estimate. He gave her a deep bow, and motioned his men to stand down, but Phatasma kept both arms extended menacingly.

"For all my years as Queen of Scoundrels, no one has ever called me your highness."

"The price for dealing with scoundrels, my fair lady."

Phatasma narrowed her eyes and looked around to assess his crew, most of which were young men and injured soldiers sent back home from the front lines.

"The queen of these waters has spoiled for a fight, and you dared deprive her of it in your cowardice?"

"Do not mistake creativity for cowardice, your highness."

"Speak then! And my golden weave better not be a simple lure."

"It is no lure."

He snapped his fingers and Phatasma turned her blade to face him, and her throwing hand to mark him as well. A group of men shuffled about below deck and returned with five crates.

"Open them." She commanded, and so they did.

As she was promised, fine Gold Weave brimmed four crates, and in the last one she saw two things. A fine violet Veran sail, incredibly expensive and difficult to come by, but more importantly, she saw a neatly rolled parchment.

"I do not like that which I do not understand, Baron." She said, then sheathed her blade finally and went to examine the parchment. "What is this?"

"A memorandum of understanding, you see, the civilised world sees you as not much more than a menace. I am inclined to believe that any woman that calls herself a queen has more decorum than she may let on. This is a proposal of an accord, Queen Phatasma."

Phatasma flashed an unsettling grin when she began to read it.

*'Oh, poor Fennyor.'*

"The thing with accords at sea…" she began as she continued to read. "You're best-off honouring them lest the waves take you, I always say."

*Scoundrels, Kings, all men must die*
*Broken wings, all birds must fly*
*Schemeless strings, say every lie*
*Golden rings, from corpses pry*
*Severed limbs, no ship sits dry*
*Tomorrow brings, no wave too high*
*Today sings, lend ear and eye*
*Of endless wins, turn ship to sky*
*With violet frills, she sails aye aye*
*Queen O' scoundrels, she sails aye aye*

Phatasma was resting brazenly at a tavern called *'Melnech's Brew'* in a nameless shanty town near Contara. She sat and listened to her own men sing terrible jingles meant to appease her, when none amongst them knew to put together anything of note.

But that was not why she was there.

She was getting more and more intoxicated as she spent more time at that establishment, but that was a side effect more so than the point of her presence on land.

The door opened violently, and the singing stopped.

*'Finally…'*

Phatasma had been there for weeks now, frequenting that tavern endlessly, until her quarry arrived.

"I hear there be a self proclaimed queen in these parts."

The voice that rumbled then scraped across ears as though it were produced from sandpaper. The owner of said voice was no less the gruesome figure either, a scar slashed across his swollen lips, thinning hair hidden under a tricorne hat. He was a larger fellow, and he reeked.

"Aye, here she be, and she is not in the business of granting an audience to beached whales." Phatasma mocked, and the man approached with his group of near twenty men.

"Not a problem then," he put his boot on her table and eyed her intently. "No beached whales far as the eye can see, but no queens either. Only cows O' the sea."

Phatasma grimaced and kicked the table into him, and immediately a brawl began. And brawls amongst scoundrels were often deadly affairs.

The large man pushed the table to one side, and half expected Phatasma to leap back into her men behind her for protection. Instead, he found himself falling to his back to avoid a daring lunge. Phatasma had lashed out at him using the table for a distraction, her sword fully extended, but he ducked out of the way and kicked at her feet as he fell.

"To the captain!"

A phrase that was echoed on both sides as scoundrel clashed into scoundrel. Rusty blades scraped into tattered ones, as two groups of underhanded men fought against each other, and somewhere in the middle of it Phatasma rolled to her feet.

The burly captain found his footing too, and in the confusion, he grabbed one of her own men, overpowering him for a moment as he pushed Phatasma's man into her. The aim was clear, to distract her as she had done with the table, and to find an opening. But the Queen of Scoundrels proved to be a heartless woman.

With a bent knee, she extended her blade into her own man's chest, skewering him and reversing his momentum to counter. Her burly opponent laughed as he jumped out of the way only to notice Phatasma was about to fling a dagger at him.

It was all he could do to grab the closest body to guard him, one of his own men this time.

"Captains! Get a damn hold of yourselves!"

Harvggad's voice grabbed the establishment by its foundations and shook it until the fighting died down.

"Things were getting interesting, must ye spoil the fun?" Desgar said, who had been merrily engaging in unarmed combat with three others. Not entirely besting them.

"Fun is for the waves, when you lot are thieving off merchants." Harvggad growled, then turned to Phatasma and the large captain.

"Aye, yer man has a head on his shoulder, *queen*."

“I’d be concerned if it were an arse, Fennyor.”

The two that had just been at each other’s throats began to laugh. Two of their own men had died needlessly, and there they were settling down into conversation over the table Phatasma had kicked down.

“This be no way to treat a queen, Fennyor. *Captain* Fennyor.” Phatasma said, and to this day it surprised Harvggad when she spoke in that manner. He had heard her speak normally to her sister, and even eloquently when she so chose, but now she regressed into sea-speak.

“Had to see for meself, what kind of queen she was.”

“Well? How was the Queen of Scoundrels then?”

“Fine. Just fine. No more, no less.” He said, and she soured her face again. “Though let it be known scoundrels are better off with a king.”

“I trust ye did not come here to trade slights,”

“Nay, been meaning to find ye, actually.”

“He talked to you too, didn’t he?”

Fennyor nodded and motioned for ale.

“Well,” Phatasma leaned back in her chair, that creaked in response. “I’ve been here sat on me arse for weeks waiting for yer generous behind to show up, I have a plan you see. But it’ll need something we’re both in short supply of.”

“And what might that be, that the *queen* of scoundrels lacks.”

“Faith in each other.”

They shared a long gaze, each studying the other for tells, each inspecting how relaxed the other was, how quickly their eyes moved, how heavily they breathed.

Then they both laughed.

“Aye, I thought so,” Phatasma said. “No faith among scoundrels. And just so. I still have a plan, though. If ye be interested.”

“Let’s hear it.”

“First, I need to know. What’d you tell him?”

“It’s them, not him. Aye, I was approached twice. A Motran and a Migoran, both tried to recruit me and my men into a joint navy they be building.”

*‘Odd. He hid Motran involvement from me. Why?’*

“And?”

“And what? Spat in their faces, naturally.”

"Good, I accepted to help them."

"Ye bloody wench!"

Phatasma rolled her eyes and poured some of her ale into his mug.

"Would I be sitting here if I meant to follow through? Ye be an honourable man or something, Fennyor?"

"Scoundrels we be, but any dealings with the crown have never paid off for us. Ever. You ought to know, princess killer in yer own right."

"The crown has never had to deal with me, so listen. They know your cove in the islands up north, and they mean to raid it when they've built enough ships. They mean for me to join them, and I will."

Fennyor glued his eyes to Phatasma as she spoke now.

"If ye think I be all looks, then think again, Captain Fennyor. I know if I sail with them to attack that cove of ye, we'd be doomed. You've five ships, none as good as Marinarma, but all better than my second best ship. The Migorans and Motrans won't have men with sea legs, and at best I expect ships that support fifty men, not three hundred."

"Aye, aye, all that I knew, so let me guess. Ye sail with them, then turn in the middle of battle? They'll see it coming two shorelines away."

"Exactly, which is why I have a plan. I'll trade ye. Two of yer ships for two of mine. That'll make ye look weaker in the cove. We lure them in, and I'll have yer two ships hidden to flank them. That way they'll be trapped in the cove with ye, and never again will land monarchs think to dip their toes into the sea."

Fennyor's brows stitched together, which made for an awful sigh for Phatasma to endure. But then he raised a finger.

"Under one condition."

"Aye?"

"The ships we swap will have mixed crews."

Phatasma narrowed her eyes, then stood up, arms folded.

"I see no harm in it. So be it."

"Ye be a dangerous lass, Phatasma. But we have an accord."

He stood up and lifted his mug, to which she picked up her own, empty as it now was.

"That we do, and ye know the thing about accords, Fennyor. They're as good as those keeping them."

*Oh joy, oh joy, to sail the blue sea*
*Oh joy, oh joy, to sail the blue sea*

*I once was a lad in the town of* ***Brisbree***
*I had a drunk father, and said he to me*

*My boy, my boy, steer clear of the sea*
*My boy, my boy, steer clear of the sea*

*I grew up a little, no longer as wee*
*But mother did grab me, and so did she plea*

*My boy, my boy, beware of the sea*
*My boy, my boy, beware of the sea*

*Scoundrels you'll meet, you'll run and you'll flee*
*They'll chase ye with daggers and murderous glee*

*My boy, my boy, abandon the sea*
*My boy, my boy, abandon the sea*

*Alone I grew older only to see*
*That the only scoundrel in this story was me!*

*Oh joy, oh joy, to plunder the sea,*
*Oh joy, oh joy, to plunder the sea.*

"Are ye sure this is how you want to do it, captain?"
"Positive."
"Captain, can I say something honest?"
"Only if you want to lose your tongue, Desgar."
"Ye be crazy, Captain."

A storm brewed on the horizon. Not a good day to be at sea, especially not off Fennyor's Cove. But the stage was set regardless, the weather was ire, and the setting was even more dire.

Fennyor's own fleet paired with *The Golden Herron* and *Hida's Revenge* and their mixed crews remained docked near shore. The island surrounding the cove was interesting in terms of features. It brandished a natural arch that was wide enough for ships to pass beneath and acted as a natural gate to the cove. From the arch a sea stack formed, and beyond it skerries that made approach from any other direction impossible. Islets and headlands broke for an estuary further down the island, but the focal point was clearly beneath the natural arch.

Phatasma had left Desgar in charge of *The Sea of Dunes*, and she had given him clear commands of what to do and when to act. Then she had given different commands to the two ships that accompanied him of Fennyor's.

Meanwhile, Phatasma's own ship made its way on its own towards the Migoran flagship. The fourth warship the Migorans had constructed, *'Liora's Plume'*.

Phatasma wore that menacing face again. Her heart drummed rhythmically in her chest, and she could not wipe away her psychotic smile. Then thunder struck in the distance, and she was spurred into action to get her ship and crew ready to crest the waves that came their way. Even the sea was ready for war.

"I leave her in yer hands Harvggad, you may be the single most trustworthy person in this entire area." Phatasma laughed as she jumped from her ship to *Liora's Plume*, leaving behind an entire crew watching her every move.

"Good to see you again, your highness." Baron Lennaz bowed.

"Aye aye, skip the pleasantries."

"Of which there were no shortage of in correspondence." He laughed as he glanced over to her ship. "That's quite the vessel. Good name too."

*'He knew Mari?'*

"Aye, but our focus is in front. See them, Baron? Sitting ducks. I told them I'd be helping them against you, and they believed my every word. Everything is ready."

"I do quite believe it is. And in this storm, best be on with it."

"Just so,"

She stood there, hands crossed, between droves of Migorans that could've apprehended her at any moment. Her ship was wedged between the two biggest vessels they brought to bear, and it still made them look like cogs. In their large group, they approached the island steadily. Phatasma fixated her gaze around, though to limited effect from the descending mist.

"Welcome! Migorans, Motrans, and all gathered!" Fennyor's voice echoed against crashing waves and thunderous skies. The Baron looked around and so did Phatasma, not knowing where the voice came from. "Welcome to my cove, the site of yer first and last tangle with scoundrels."

No sooner had he ended his words did their ships rock violently. Rocks were being flung at them from beyond the mist, from the top of the headlands that adorned the coast.

"To be expected, men! Steady the course! Soon we will be upon them, and they will have no reprieve!" The baron yelled confidently.

"There's one small detail that had escaped me, Baron."

Phatasma spoke slowly and the Baron narrowed his eyes towards her.

"My lord! It's them that're on us!"

At that exact moment, Phatasma flung one dagger after the other at the man that stood no more than two arms' lengths away. Both her daggers struck, and the man fell to his knees, clutching at his neck.

"That's the thing with accords..." she said, then her entire crew stormed the deck as she plucked the daggers from his neck.

Fighting broke out everywhere.

They had reached just below the natural arch when Fennyor's ships attacked from the side, when Phatasma chose to strike. But not Desgar, oddly enough. Arrows flew everywhere, men boarded ships until they lost track whose vessel they were aboard. It was utter chaos, and to add to it, Fennyor began dropping rocks from atop the arch, sinking ships aplenty.

The Motran and Migoran force that had been sent to subdue the scoundrels would undoubtedly be decimated. But Phatasma had her eyes out for more. She went back to her ship and recalled her men, and in a show of treachery, she ordered a firing of her two mangonels at the natural arch.

"Phatasma, ye bloody..."

"What? Scoundrel?! Hah!" Phatasma laughed openly as Fennyor lost his voice and regrouped. The arch was standing still, and from above he owned an advantage against Phatasma's ship, but the chaos had been redoubled as now crewmates turned against each other.

Then Desgar showed up from the other side of the island, and rammed into one of Fennyor's ships, breaking it at the centre, as he too joined the fray.

*'There is only one way to end this.'*

Phatasma picked her way from ship to ship, dancing between combatants, flinging daggers at those that came at her, then collecting them in one fluid motion as she made for the cove itself.

"Desgar! Captains! With me! Harvggad, the outside is yours!"

Together with a motley bunch, she stormed Fennyor's cove, which was not as well entrenched as the exterior was. After all, they did not expect to need to fight on land.

But even in this, Phatasma was ever the scoundrel. Leaving her men to fight just so she could get to Fennyor at the top of the arch. She only stopped once, only to make Desgar dismantle a fishing net of sorts, then eventually, she reached the summit.

Phatasma and Desgar approached, but only Phatasma had the insanity to leap onto the narrow shelf of the shaky arch in thunder and rain, to fight a man twice her size.

"Yer a damn bloody woman alright, Phatasma! Beat me to it!"

"Don't ye worry, Fennyor, I'll take good care of yer fleet."

Phatasma approached, picking her steps as she let fly a dagger at Fennyor's feet. The man's movements were more deliberate than in the tavern. One slipup and he would surely fall. He was ready for Phatasma's tricks, or so he thought.

Their swords clashed atop the arch, and Phatasma's jabs were quick and plenty. She did not possess the power to match Fennyor, so she kept him busy. Until once again, she flung a dagger at him, but Fennyor was wise to it still.

*'One more time. He should get it.'*

Another flurry of blows was traded, sparks flew between their blades as lightning lit up the sky, then she reached for a dagger and extended a hand to throw it, only to feel Fennyor's cold grip on her arm.

"Desgar, now!"

She cried and let herself fall with her legs spread to wrap them around the narrow arch. Fennyor was about to pull her up when he got tangled up in the net Desgar had plucked. Then, Desgar pulled on it, and Fennyor slipped and could only catch the side of the arch, hanging from it from one side.

Phatasma cackled as she pushed herself up and stood over his hand. She had an unsettling glisten in her eyes as she looked at Fennyor.

"I yield! Damn it, Phatasma. The Scoundrels have a queen! Help me up! I'll serve ye as well as any of them!"

Phatasma seemed to have been ready to have Desgar pull him up, but the way he spoke, it almost made her feel as though he expected this. Her face soured again.

"I have no need for a weak king. The Queen of Scoundrels rules alone."

"Phatasma! Ye mad wench, wait!"

"O bountiful sea that has given much to me, I praise thee and return thine whale free!" She proclaimed, and in one motion, sliced his fingers off, letting him drop with a massive thud and crash into one of his ships below. "Migorans! Motrans! Scoundrels! Drop yer weapons! There's only one queen in these waters, and to cross her is to cross the sea!"

The weather only deteriorated further as she spoke, but in spite of every cloud in the sky, the outcome was clear as day. On that day, Phatasma took in many of the sailors that had been sent to subdue her, and she bartered away any that held rank. Her fleet doubled in size, and truly she was crowned as Queen of the Scoundrels.

*'That's the thing with accords. They're all bloody useless.'*

## For Self

### 16th OF THIRD WINTER 485 F.O.

The Marinarma's Ambition was docked off the coast of the Migoran town of Nosfara. The ship rocked gently in the still shallow waters of the coastline; anchored such that it would remain hidden from prying eyes.

"That's twelve you've gone through so far, Captain."

"I thought you said you couldn't count past ten, Desgar."

"Necessity breeds innovation, aye?"

"Words I did not think I would hear strung from your mouth."

Desgar laughed, and Phatasma smiled beneath her hat. She had been lying on her back in her bed, hands behind her head, one knee bent and the other over it.

At this point in time, Phatasma was lavished with plunder. Her claim of queenhood could not have been less disputed, especially as she looked more exotic and flamboyant than any queen that had ever ruled in Osgara. She adorned her hair with golden threads that kept its shape and glistened whenever light struck her hair. Her eyes had gone completely violet, and she had painted her eyelids a dark shade and better defined her brows.

Her arms were a litter of bracelets lined with many gems and precious stones, down to her fingers each carrying a multitude of rings. Her feet saw their own measure of anklets as well, but only when she had no need of her boots. The one aspect of her that remained true to her fiendish nature was her brazen choice of clothing, which had only grown less modest.

But now she was on her back, and her tricorne hat covered her face, still adorned in Liora's feather.

"Just send in the next one, Desgar."

"Captain, might I be honest?"

"No, but you always are anyway, for some reason. Perhaps a disdain for that tongue I never pluck out."

"We ought to sail west, captain."

"Hm?"

"You've done everything there is to be done in the east. We've been living on years old plunder like kings thanks to you. And ye know the lads would follow you wherever."

"Quaint. Desgar, do you perhaps recall the name of this ship?"

Desgar raised a brow at her accent and tone of voice. It was almost as if Phatasma, the Queen of Scoundrels, was resting, and an old shadow of Paranessa managed a conversation.

"I have not taken to calling it Marinarma's Ambition out of some hollow sense of atonement, no. Her ambition and mine are well entwined, they are by many measures one and the same."

Desgar remained silent, wearing only an impressed smile. Proud almost. That after years of company, he finally had a passing moment to learn about the woman behind the mask of the violet scourge of the sea.

"Desgar, I've done heinous things. And will continue to do so unapologetically. I am well beyond all illusion of painting my actions as just, or thinly veiling my reasons. I have a dream, Desgar. And I once thought that riches would ferry me towards it. But no. Gold and precious trinkets are as useful as froth on the waves."

"Bwoah, I wouldn't say that now, captain."

She puffed air out of her nose and shook her head under the hat.

"That dream of yours, captain. What's stopping ye?"

"The world."

"Hah?"

"Forget it, Desgar. I need someone that knows about ship building, adverse weather, the deep sea, the stars, the wind, and preferably some manner of magic whilst I am listing wants."

"Is that the bounty we put out?"

Phatasma nodded, still hiding under the hat.

"Ten thousand Lots, for all that? I should start learning."

"The sea will have dried by then," she said.

Desgar laughed and turned to look outside her cabin.

"Ten thousand Lots, is a lot of Lots, captain."

"I'd sell myself to such a man, if he existed."

"Might be a lass, captain."

"Then I'd sell you, but you'd like that, wouldn't you? Utter scoundrel."

"And ye asked me why I swam back for ye?"

Phatasma chuckled and plucked her hat to pop it onto her head.

"I truly did need a friend, didn't I? I was far too blind to see it. Thank you, Desgar. I owe you more than gold can repay."

Desgar gave Phatasma the strangest look of concern then.

"What're ye waiting for, ye sea dog?" She barked and tossed a goblet at him, which he deftly dodged. "Go fetch me the next one, and if I don't find what I'm after, it'll be your head that's our new bowsprit figurchcad."

"Aye aye, captain!" Desgar scurried out of the cabin, leaving Phatasma to reach for one of her beloved throwing knives. She glanced at it as she turned it in her hands while she waited.

*'How many lives have you taken? And just how good have I got at tossing you into innocent lives? And what is it with me and this meek tone? Has gold and fame truly softened me? Or is it the work of age?'*

Desgar tossed a man into her cabin and closed the door immediately, leaving Phatasma to look up and inspect the man. A plump fellow with short hair, cleanly shaven, wearing a long robe, and seemed to carry with him a collection of tomes.

"Sit."

"Ah, certainly." He quickly obeyed, and Phatasma scowled.

"Look at my study, what do you see?"

"Er, a moment." He picked up the parchment left there and began to inspect the drawings and labels upon it. "Oh, quite fascinating. A ship design. Quite innovative if I may say so. These kinds of masts, and the materials you wish to make them from, this is excellent work this."

"You reckon it can be made?"

"Oh, of course! With this, why, a vessel like this would perhaps take you twice as far as this one might, or indeed any I've seen built. It is exquisite design, yes, this must have taken years of research to-"

The man's body dropped, and blood leaked from his neck as he choked on his last words. Phatasma's aim had rarely let her down, and her violet eyes seemed to glisten after every knife she threw to take a life.

*'Bloody sycophant.'*

"Bring in the damned next one."

*'I have an entire crew to sample my behind... What I need is someone to push progress... not this.'*

"I say, unhand me!" A voice grumbled as Desgar coarsely shoved the next man in. "Must you shove and push? I own two feet just as you do."

Desgar shot the man a venomous gaze, and Phatasma stifled a laugh. The man dusted himself off and looked around the room, only to see a dead man and Phatasma playing with a knife on her bed. The man promptly turned to Desgar in the doorway once more.

"Ah, good sir, you appear to have shoved me into the wrong room. I was told a man of wit was needed, not, eh, whatever he was meant to be."

The door closed, and the man shook his head.

This one was an interesting specimen. He did not look older than his mid-twenties perhaps, and yet his hair was white as snow, and his eyes were an unsettlingly enchanting silver. He carried himself with purpose and carried every hallmark of a very well-travelled man. Bits and pieces of his clothing showing elements of all five realms.

"Very well, might as well do this properly," he cleared his throat. "I am **Vareyan**, a wandering scholar in pursuit of my own queries that require your generous funding. What might the Queen of Scoundrels desire with a man such as myself?"

"Ye come to my ship seeking my riches, and then introduce yourself with your own queries? Ye mad?"

Vareyan was more concerned about the knife in her hand that she kept toying with than to respond, but his eyes caught the parchment on the desk.

"Of course, how could I? The needs of the lady must trump my own for the time being, I suppose. Say, are these ship schematic documents?"

Acting on impulse, he wandered towards the study and took extreme caution to not touch the dead man's body. Phatasma eyed him curiously as he studied her drawings. Then he frowned.

"Oh, I see." He offered some feigned laugher. "This is some mockery of a drawing, a joke perhaps. Though a very serious one, the drawing itself is extremely detailed, though whatever that is meant to be would sink the day it was launched into sea."

He made an effort to laugh again, though he clearly did not find it funny.

"Open the drawer, the second one. Yes, that one. Pick up that stack, find the very last page, and examine it. And do make an effort to guard your tongue, *wandering scholar*."

Vareyan studied that one as well, then paused and frowned.

He did not ask for permission. He simply plucked at a quill and found an inkwell. Phatasma raised her brows but let him act as he pleased, thinking this was his way of jesting. Until he began to modify her own drawings.

She pushed herself up, knife in hand, and approached her study, then leaned behind him, placing her head next to his eerily as he worked.

"Yes, perhaps... though... not quite... Ah- Excuse me?"

He jumped back to one side when he saw her face.

"Did I give you permission to modify *my* schematic?"

"Ah, yes, of course. Well, Queen Scoundrel, I can save you the trouble of pursuing that pattern. I doubt it would ever work."

"Why?"

"Why? Why would it work? The materials in question solve an issue for rigidity that does not exist in any waters known to any decent scholar. But allow me to humour you, for in using them you sacrifice buoyancy and stability. I can see the attempts at changing the shape and hollowing areas to solve the issue for buoyancy. But in so doing, you have sabotaged rigidity and balance. Also, just by looking at these designs, I can surmise you intend to go into uncharted waters. If so, I would mark the ship on its side, here and here, for example. That way you will always know-"

"How much cargo I can carry, yes I had a similar thought before. But, wait. Are you quite certain about these materials?"

"Well, it was a rough estimate, but whatever gain you might make in using such reinforced materials, you will quickly lose in other places. I might have a different suggestion, though the more I think about it, the less humane it may sound."

"Well... go on."

"Right, scoundrels and such. How silly of me? The suggestion is very simply to add stabilisers, here and here, but you will need people to operate them when waters become rough. And to know how to turn them. Another idea I spotted in one of your other drawings that seemed strange is this tip here, beneath the stern."

"Oh, truly?!" Phatasma almost leapt.

"I would need time to study it, but it holds *some* promise, yes. Though these are only marginal benefits. I'm afraid that to answer a quandary, I will need fuller details."

"Just how do you know all this?" Phatasma found herself asking, still leaning over to study his quick sketches. The joy she felt then she had not known since she had left her home and had lost her first love. This man knew more than she did about the things that ate away at her mind, and he willingly divulged out of nothing but the sheer pursuit of knowledge.

"Queen Scoundrel, I will have you know I am not just *any* self proclaimed scholar. I did not write up a tome featuring one flimsy hypothesis which I claim to have verified myself and called myself a learned man because of it. Oh no. I have travelled this world, many times over. No rock I've left unturned in my search for knowledge, no tome untouched, no matter how mad the rambler."

"But you must have a love for the sea, to know so much about ship making, do you not?"

"I detest the sea. But out of respect for your knife, perhaps I ought to *guard my tongue*. Queen Scoundrel."

"Phatasma, just call me Phatasma. For a well-learned man, you are ill acquainted with formalities."

"Oh, I have little love for manufactured nobilities, either. The pompous nerve of men and women to think they were born better than others. It irks me to no end, Qu- Phatasma. Though your title is at least one you have forged for yourself. And I do not mean that as a compliment, for to be a queen of scoundrels is a... well, a goal none should strive towards."

"On that, we agree."

*'After all I have done... could this world smile upon me yet?'*

"I must say, you are far more pleasant than I was led to believe. Though, my colleague here might not agree."

Vareyan shuffled away from the body as best he could, and Phatasma laughed and sat herself next to Vareyan on the cramped chair.

"This is, hardly appropriate, my- er- Phatasma."

"Ye forget what kind of lass I be, Vareyan lover of land?"

"Ah, so it *was* manufactured. I knew you couldn't have actually sounded like that."

"And why might that be?"

She eyed him with big violet eyes. She could not have known it at the time, but she had every hint of star-struck eyes as she watched Vareyan.

"Have you heard your man out there? He clearly knows no other tongue. Yours was far more pronounced, clearly well practised, but exactly that. He makes mistakes that you do not, but I suppose you are pulling out parchments for my ideas on ships, not accents."

"The smartest man I have had under this roof."

"Forgive me if that does not stir my fancy."

"Hah. Well said."

"But you have not yet responded to my question. What kind of waters are you preparing to voyage through?"

"You will not believe me if I merely tell you. Tomorrow we shall set sail, and I shall show you. Lover of land."

"I beseech you, stop calling me that."

"The lover of land detests his new name?"

Vareyan sighed, and Phatasma continued to search through her parchments.

"What is out there that you wish to travel so far into the sea to retrieve?" Vareyan asked abruptly, which took Phatasma off guard.

"A dream..."

*'Really? Is that what I just said?'*

"Captain! Next one be ready for ye."

"Oh, I be happy with this one, Desgar. Toss the rest overboard."

"Slightly excessive, after all, I've not yet proven myself on matters of weather. I assure you I am a terrible sailor and-"

Phatasma embraced him and kissed him abruptly.

The Queen of Scoundrels had often done much worse than a kiss to unsettle a man, and yet for the first time in many years, she had been genuine. He came to her in a moment of weakness, and held every promise she could've asked of him, even his hatred for nobility.

He plucked at heartstrings she had once thought were beyond repair, and yet, there she was, making a fool of herself.

*'Oh, how cheaply I sell myself, and yet... Perhaps even I can...'*

Echoes of her sister's last words to her came flooding into her mind, and Phatasma pulled away from Vareyan. She bit her lips and held back tears as those words of condemnation did not cease.

"For all my knowledge..." she heard Vareyan mutter beneath his breath, as he was clearly unsure of how to handle her. One of the most dangerous women alive had simultaneously kissed him and broken down next to him.

"I fear I may never understand a woman's heart."

At that, Phatasma could not help but laugh and weep at the same time. She tossed the dagger away and turned back to embrace Vareyan. A quiet resolution within her to prove her sister's words wrong grew steadily. A fierce desire to begin anew swelled within her, even as a corpse remained warm beneath her seat. And she anchored all these hopes around a man she had just met.

Such was the life of a woman that had left home on impulse.

"Vareyan?"

"Y-yes?"

"If you ever speak of this to anyone out of this room..."

"You'll have my tongue?"

"And so much more, Vary."

# Without Remorse

## 29th OF SECOND SPRING 485 F.O.
## DEAR FATHER & DEAREST MOTHER

I have wronged you beyond all words.

I do not pretend nor think that I can have your love again.

But I wished at least to let these letters wet this parchment with my remorse for my actions. You bear no fault of what I have done. Nothing you did, no matter how extreme, justifies what I have gone on to do.

I cannot claim either to know if you care for what has become of me, but I seek to tell you, regardless. Perhaps one or both of you might wish to know what their own blood has become.

Riches I have attained beyond many monarchs. Fame, I have also garnered more than I had hoped, but these were simple things to find.

I have found a man who both of you would have fiercely approved of. Though perhaps his tongue might have slipped here or there. He is fiercely quick witted; he is well versed in many domains of knowledge beyond my reckoning. And I suspect his is of noble northern blood that you would have celebrated.

He is a blessing, one that has given me hope to begin anew.

Perhaps it is not too late for me yet.

Also, I have learned of what ill fate has befallen your noble status, but let it be known that no mother nor father of mine shall live without honour. I've sent a sum with this letter that ought to see you through many years, and I have resolved to continue to do so.

*Paranessa, perhaps once more.*

# Appendix

## Ships of the Gaudy Coast

## Marinarma's Ambition

Captain: **Phatasma, The Queen of Scoundrels**
Classification: **Flagship** / Affiliation: **Herself**

## Hida's Revenge

Captain: **Norlac, Quartermaster of no Quarter**
Classification: **Ancillary** / Affiliation: **Captain Phatasma**

## The Sea of Dunes

Captain: **Myures, Wave of Darkness**
Classification: **Raider** / Affiliation: **Captain Phatasma**

## The Golden Heron

Captain: **Dengal, Din of Despair**
Classification: **Raider** / Affiliation: **Captain Phatasma**

## Anchored Light

Captain: **Fennyor, Binder of the Waves**
Classification: **Flagship** / Affiliation: **Himself**

## The Bound Crescent

Captain: **Ginnerec, Mind of Night**
Classification: **Ancillary** / Affiliation: **Captain Fennyor**

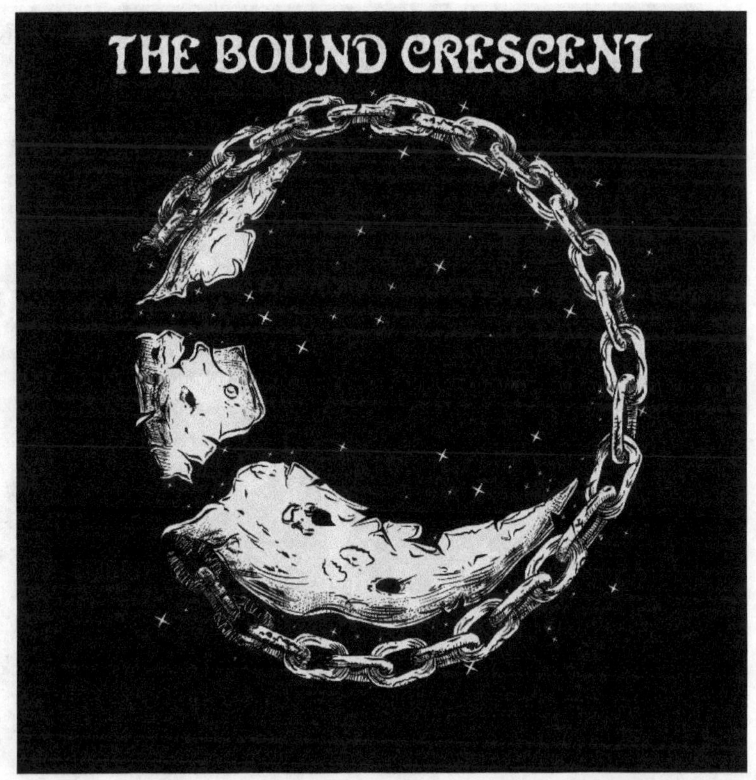

## The Shackled Star

Captain: **Yolz, First Seakin**
Classification: **Fighter** / Affiliation: **Captain Fennyor**

## The Clasped Blade

Captain: **Mellek, Ralm of the Sea**
Classification: **Fighter** / Affiliation: **Captain Fennyor**

## Chained Fate

Captain: **Cenlam, Crier of Contara**
Classification: **Raider** / Affiliation: **Captain Fennyor**

## Tulip's Tendrils

Captain: **Baron Anyov Mer'Lintha Ral'Throia**
Classification: **Warship** / Affiliation: **Migora**

## Liora's Plume

Captain: **Baron Lennaz Mer'Ginliya Ral'Throia**
Classification: **Warship** / Affiliation: **Migora**

## Solar Pillar

Captain: **Ilyon Seakin**
Classification: **Warship** / Affiliation: **Motra**

# Acknowledgement

While we certainly enjoy creating and telling stories in Osgara, and wish to do so even more often! These Novellas we write for those that choose to support us.

It is the least we could do to honour your contributions here, such that your names be immortalised in these works of fiction. You are and will forever be, a part of this.

To the first of hopefully many:

***Mohammed Kapiel***

www.ingramcontent.com/pod-product-compliance
Lightning Source LLC
LaVergne TN
LVHW052009160826
845678LV00005B/1697

* 9 7 8 3 9 1 1 1 1 1 1 5 7 *